WARRIORS

RAVENPAW'S PATH

#1: SHATTERED PEACE

WARRIORS

RAVENPAW'S PATH

#1: SHATTERED PEACE

CREATED BY
ERIN HUNTER

WRITTEN BY
DAN JOLLEY

ART BY
JAMES L. BARRY

HAMBURG // LONDON // LOS ANGELES // TOKYO

HARPER
An Imprint of HarperCollinsPublishers

Warriors: Ravenpaw's Path Vol. 1:
Shattered Peace
Created by Erin Hunter
Written by Dan Jolley
Art by James L. Barry

Digital Tones - Lincy Chan
Lettering - Lucas Rivera
Cover Design - Louis Csontos

Editor - Jenna Winterberg
Managing Editor - Vy Nguyen
Print-Production Manager - Lucas Rivera
Art Director - Al-Insan Lashley
Director of Sales and Manufacturing - Allyson DeSimone
Associate Publisher - Marco Pavia
President and C.O.O. - John Parker
C.E.O. and Chief Creative Officer - Stu Levy

A **TOKYOPOP** Manga

TOKYOPOP and ⟨⟩ are trademarks or registered trademarks of TOKYOPOP Inc.

TOKYOPOP Inc.
5900 Wilshire Blvd. Suite 2000
Los Angeles, CA 90036

E-mail: info@TOKYOPOP.com
Come visit us online at www.TOKYOPOP.com

For information address HarperCollins Children's Books, a division of HarperCollins Publishers,
10 East 53rd Street, New York, NY 10022.
www.harpercollinschildrens.com

ISBN 978-0-06-168865-2
Library of Congress catalog card number: 2009920733

09   10   11   12   13   LP/WOR   10   9   8   7   6   5   4   3   2   1
❖
First Edition

Hello!

Who would have guessed that Ravenpaw's decision to leave ThunderClan and live with the loner Barley in the Twoleg barn would have prompted such a storm of protest? Not from his Clanmates—although Firestar and Graystripe were sad to see him go, they knew he would never be happy in the Clan—but from all the readers for whom Ravenpaw was the cat they most wanted to see become a warrior and take revenge upon his bullying mentor, Tigerclaw.

I have lost count of the number of times I've been asked what Ravenpaw's warrior name would have been. My reply is always: He was never going to have one! Ravenpaw's strength lies in his quiet sense of self, which is the kind of strength that needs space to develop, away from the pressures of Clan life with all its rules, tasks, and expectations. Safe on the farm with Barley, Ravenpaw has become confident, relaxed, and a friendly host to Clan cats passing by on their way to the Moonstone.

But I knew that life would never be quite so simple for Ravenpaw as moving to the farm and instantly forgetting his upbringing. He is forest-born, and has the instincts of every Clan cat—the strength and hope that comes with loyalty to the warrior code, the certainty that there will always be cats you can call upon when times get hard. Ravenpaw and Barley have a good life together, but when everything is turned upside down by the arrival of coldhearted rogues, Ravenpaw's instincts kick in—and suddenly he is forced to ask himself: Am I still a member of ThunderClan?

Best wishes always,
Erin Hunter

THINGS ARE VERY SIMPLE HERE.

SLEEP, HUNT, EAT...

NOT THAT I REALLY HAVE TO HUNT, NOT WITH ALL THE MICE IN THE BARN.

8

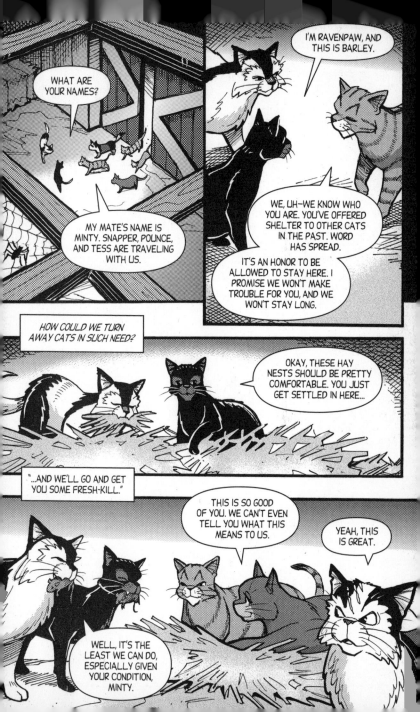

IT'S REALLY LUCKY WILLIE AND HIS FRIENDS FIND US WHEN THEY DO.

THEY'VE BARELY EVEN FINISHED THEIR FRESH-KILL...

...WHEN MINTY GIVES BIRTH.

EVERYONE...

...THIS IS SNOWFLAKE, AND ICICLE, AND CLOUDY, AND SNIFF.

I CAN'T TAKE MY EYES OFF THEM. I'VE...I'VE JUST FORGOTTEN.

FORGOTTEN HOW BEAUTIFUL KITS CAN BE-LIKE THE KITS BACK IN THUNDERCLAN.

OUR VISITORS SETTLE IN FOR A FEW DAYS, SPENDING ALL THEIR TIME TAKING CARE OF THE KITS.

BARLEY AND I ARE MORE THAN HAPPY TO DO THEIR HUNTING FOR THEM.

RAVENPAW, YOU'RE BACK!

LOOK, KITTENS! RAVENPAW'S BRINGING FOOD FOR US!

HE'S LETTING ME MAKE PLENTY OF MILK FOR YOU!

MEEP!

THE VISITORS ALWAYS HIDE FROM THE TWOLEGS. I TRY TO TELL THEM IT'S OKAY, BUT THEY'RE FIRM ABOUT IT.

IT REALLY IS ALL RIGHT. THEY WON'T BOTHER US.

I'M SORRY, RAVENPAW, IT'S JUST...WE'VE HAD SOME BAD EXPERIENCES WITH TWOLEGS.

OLD HABITS DIE HARD, YOU KNOW.

27

WHAT IF BARLEY IS RIGHT? WHAT IF I AM A CLAN CAT, DEEP DOWN?

I DON'T KNOW. THE ONLY THING I DO KNOW...

...IS THAT I MISS THOSE KITS SO MUCH THAT IT'S KILLING ME.

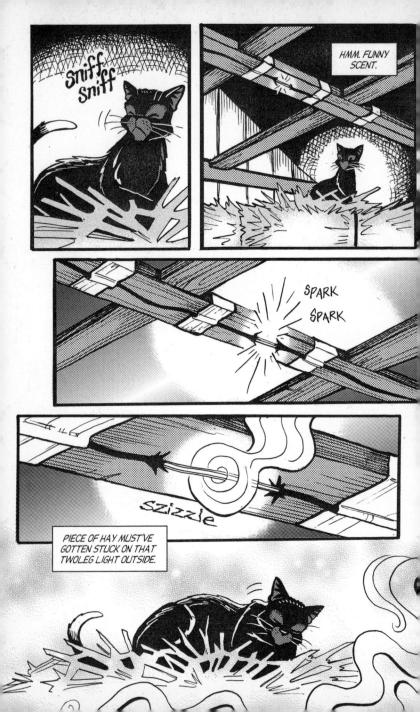

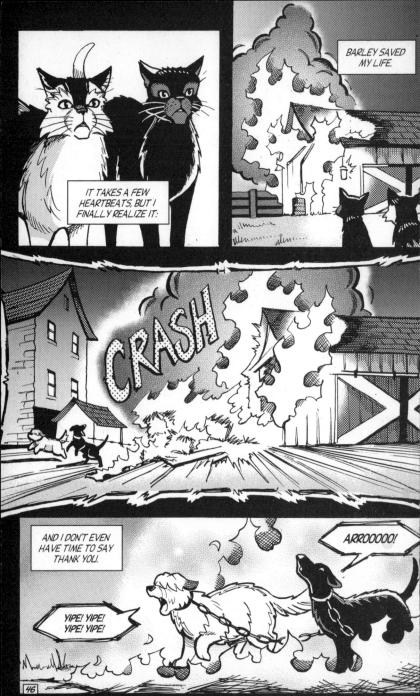

THE REST OF THE NIGHT IS PRETTY MISERABLE.

SEEING AS THE COWS AREN'T USING IT, WE SNEAK INTO THEIR PLACE...

...AND CURL UP AS BEST WE CAN. THE HAY IS DIRTY AND SMELLS LIKE COW POOP.

BUT WE ARE BOTH TOO TIRED TO CARE.

HE NEXT FEW DAYS ARE TOUGH.
THE BARN IS STILL STANDING, YES–
FLAP FLAP FLAPETTA
–BUT IT IS TOO WRECKED TO USE AS A PROPER HOME.
NOT TO MENTION, THE THING THE TWOLEGS PUT ACROSS THE TOP MAKES SO MUCH NOISE–
–IT'S SCARED ALMOST ALL THE MICE AWAY.

THE REALIZATION IS SO PAINFUL THAT IT FEELS LIKE MY HEAD'S GOING TO SPLIT IN HALF.

BARLEY WAS RIGHT. FROM THE VERY BEGINNING, HE WAS RIGHT.

AND I'VE BEEN SUCH A FOOL.

WHAT EXACTLY ARE YOU LOOKING FOR UP HERE, ANYWAY?

THIS.

THIS IS THE TUNNEL TO THE MOONSTONE.

AND...THAT'S WHAT, AGAIN? REMIND ME.

THE FIRST TIME I CAME HERE, I WAS WITH DUSTPAW AND SANDPAW.

THEY WERE SO EXCITED ABOUT THE POSSIBILITY OF SHARING TONGUES WITH STARCLAN...WE ALL WERE.

I LET BARLEY KNOW THAT THE MOONSTONE IS SACRED TO THE CLANS. IT'S WHERE LEADERS COME TO GET THEIR NINE LIVES...

...AND WHERE THE MEDICINE CATS MEET EACH HALF-MOON TO TALK TO THEIR WARRIOR ANCESTORS IN THEIR DREAMS.

EVERY CLAN APPRENTICE MAKES THE JOURNEY ONCE. IT'S A RITUAL, A PART OF BEING A CLAN CAT.

THERE'S HARDLY ANY LIGHT. EVEN STRAINING TO LOOK, I CAN BARELY SEE ANYTHING.

BUT I KNOW WHERE WE ARE. I KNOW WHAT THAT IS, WAITING THERE IN THE CHAMBER.

WOW. IT'S REALLY DARK IN HERE.

I MEAN, THERE'S DARK, AND THEN THERE'S *THIS.* I CAN'T TELL IF MY EYES ARE OPEN OR CLOSED.

WELL, THIS IS THE PLACE. THIS IS WHERE WE WANT TO BE.

JUST—JUST FIND A DRY SPOT AND GET SOME SLEEP, ALL RIGHT?

OH, BELIEVE ME.

FALLING ASLEEP TONIGHT... THAT'S NOT GOING TO BE A PROBLEM.

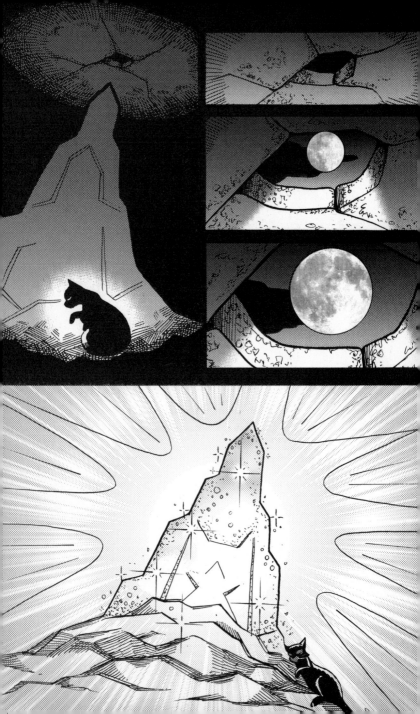

ERIN HUNTER

is inspired by a love of cats and a
fascination with the ferocity of the
natural world. As well as having
great respect for nature in all its
forms, Erin enjoys creating rich,
mythical explanations for animal
behavior. She is also the author of
the Seekers series.

Visit the Clans online
and play Warriors games at
www.warriorcats.com.

For exclusive information on your
favorite authors and artists, visit
www.authortracker.com.

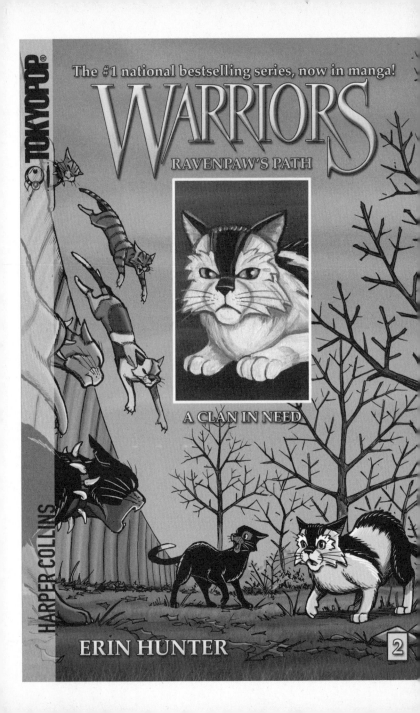

KEEP WATCH FOR

WARRIORS

RAVENPAW'S PATH

#2: A CLAN IN NEED

Ravenpaw and Barley have been driven away from their farm by a group of vicious cats. Now the two loners turn to ThunderClan—led by Ravenpaw's friend Firestar—for shelter. Firestar promises to help them take back their home as soon as possible, but ThunderClan is in great danger. BloodClan cats have been launching raids on ThunderClan's territory and attacking Clan patrols. Can Ravenpaw and Barley help Firestar and his Clan fight off their enemies? And will they ever be able to get home again?

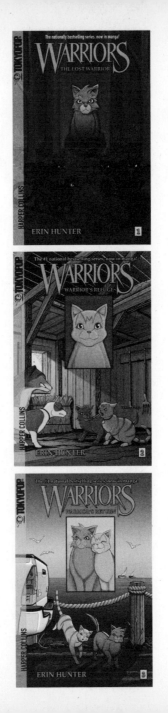

THE LOST WARRIOR

WARRIOR'S REFUGE

WARRIOR'S RETURN

Find out what really happened to Graystripe when he was captured by Twolegs, and follow him and Millie on their torturous journey through the old forest territory and Twolegplace to find ThunderClan.

The #1 national bestselling series, now in manga!

WARRIORS

TIGERSTAR & SASHA

INTO THE WOODS

ERIN HUNTER

HARPER COLLINS

TOKYOPOP

1

The #1 national bestselling series, now in manga

WARRIORS

TIGERSTAR & SASHA

ESCAPE FROM
THE FOREST

ERIN HUNTER

HARPER COLLINS

TOKYOPOP

2

The #1 national bestselling series, now in manga!

WARRIORS

TIGERSTAR & SASHA

RETURN TO THE CLANS

ERIN HUNTER

HARPER COLLINS

TOKYOPOP

3

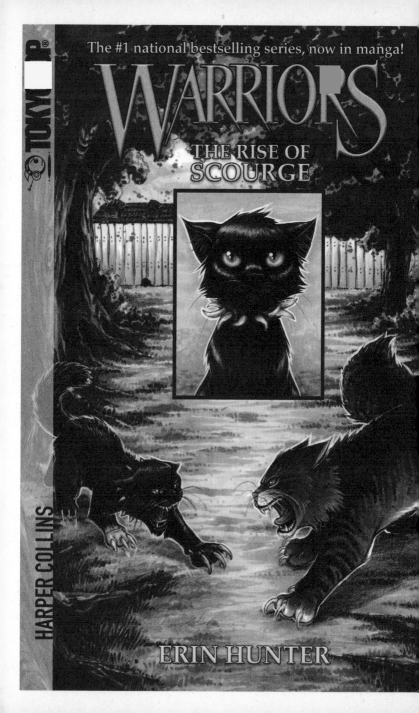

THE RISE OF
SCOURGE

Black-and-white Tiny may be the runt of the litter, but he's also the most curious about what lies beyond the backyard fence. When he crosses paths with some wild cats defending their territory, Tiny is left with scars—and a bitter, deep-seated grudge—that he carries with him back to Twolegplace. As his reputation grows among the strays and loners that live in the dirty brick alleyways, Tiny leaves behind his name, his kittypet past, and everything that was once important to him—except his deadly desire for revenge.

OMEN OF THE STARS

WARRIORS

THE FOURTH APPRENTICE

ERIN HUNTER

TURN THE PAGE FOR A PEEK AT
THE NEXT WARRIORS NOVEL,

OMEN OF THE STARS #1:
THE FOURTH APPRENTICE

Jayfeather and Lionblaze are prophesied to be two of
three cats to hold the power of the stars in their paws.
Now, they must wait for a sign from StarClan to tell
them which of their Clanmates will complete the
prophecy. Soon, a StarClan warrior will visit a new
ThunderClan apprentice—and the lives of the three
chosen cats will be forever linked.

A full moon floated in a cloudless sky, casting thick black shadows across the island. The leaves of the Great Oak rustled in a hot breeze. Crouched between Sorreltail and Graystripe, Lionblaze felt as though he couldn't get enough air.

"You'd think it would be cooler at night," he grumbled.

"I know," Graystripe sighed, shifting uncomfortably on the dry, powdery soil. "This season just gets hotter and hotter. I can't even remember when it last rained."

Lionblaze stretched up to peer over the heads of the other cats at his brother, Jayfeather, who was sitting with the medicine cats. Onestar had just reported the death of Barkface, and Kestrelflight, the remaining WindClan medicine cat, looked rather nervous to be representing his Clan alone for the first time.

"Jayfeather says StarClan hasn't told him anything about the drought," Lionblaze mewed to Graystripe. "I wonder if any of the other medicine cats—"

He broke off as Firestar, the leader of ThunderClan, rose to his paws on the branch where he had been sitting while he waited for his turn to speak. RiverClan's leader, Leopardstar, glanced up from the branch just below, where she was crouching. Onestar, the leader of WindClan, was perched in the fork of a bough a few tail-lengths higher, while ShadowClan's leader, Blackstar, was visible just as a gleam of eyes among the clustering leaves above Onestar's branch.

"Like every other Clan, ThunderClan is troubled by the heat," Firestar began. "But we are coping well. Two of our apprentices have been made into warriors and received their warrior names: Toadstep and Rosepetal."

Lionblaze sprang to his paws. "Toadstep! Rosepetal!" he yowled. The rest of ThunderClan joined in, along with several cats from WindClan and ShadowClan, though Lionblaze noticed that the RiverClan warriors were silent, looking on with hostility in their eyes.

Who ruffled their fur? he wondered. It was mean-spirited for a whole Clan to refuse to greet a new warrior at a Gathering. He twitched his ears. He wouldn't forget this the next time Leopardstar announced a new RiverClan appointment.

The two new ThunderClan warriors ducked their heads in embarrassment, though their eyes shone as they were welcomed by the Clans. Cloudtail, Toadstep's former mentor, was puffed up with pride, while Squirrelflight, who had mentored Rosepetal, watched the young warriors with gleaming eyes.

"I'm still surprised Firestar picked Squirrelflight to be a mentor," Lionblaze muttered to himself. "After she told all those lies about us being her kits."

"Firestar knows what he's doing," Graystripe responded; Lionblaze winced as he realized the gray warrior had overheard every word of his criticism. "He trusts Squirrelflight, and he wants to show every cat that she's a good warrior and a valued member of ThunderClan."

"I suppose you're right." Lionblaze blinked miserably. He had loved and respected Squirrelflight so much when he thought she was his mother, but now he felt cold and empty when he looked at her. She had betrayed him, and his littermates, too deeply for forgiveness. Hadn't she?

"If you've quite finished . . . " Leopardstar spoke over the last of the yowls of welcome and rose to her paws, fixing Firestar with a glare. "RiverClan still has a report to make."

Firestar dipped his head courteously to the RiverClan leader and took a pace back, sitting down again with his tail wrapped around his paws. "Go ahead, Leopardstar."

The RiverClan leader was the last to speak at the Gathering; Lionblaze had seen her tail twitching impatiently while the other leaders made their reports. Now her piercing gaze traveled across the cats crowded together in the clearing, while her neck fur bristled in fury.

"Prey-stealers!" she hissed.

"What?" Lionblaze sprang to his paws; his startled yowl was lost in the clamor as more cats from ThunderClan, WindClan, and ShadowClan leaped up to protest.

Leopardstar stared down at them, teeth bared, making no attempt to quell the tumult. Instinctively Lionblaze glanced upward, but there were no clouds to cover the moon;

StarClan wasn't showing any anger at the outrageous accusation. *As if any of the other Clans would want to steal slimy, stinky fish!*

He noticed for the first time how thin the RiverClan leader looked, her bones sharp as flint beneath her dappled fur. The other RiverClan warriors were the same, Lionblaze realized, glancing around; even thinner than his own Clanmates and the ShadowClan warriors—and even thinner than the WindClan cats, who looked skinny when they were full-fed.

"They're starving . . . " he murmured.

"We're all starving," Graystripe retorted.

Lionblaze let out a sigh. What the gray warrior said was true. In ThunderClan they had been forced to hunt and train at dawn and dusk in order to avoid the scorching heat of the day. In the hours surrounding sunhigh, the cats spent their time curled up sleeping in the precious shade at the foot of the walls of the stone hollow. For once the Clans were at peace, though Lionblaze suspected it was only because they were all too weak to fight, and no Clan had any prey worth fighting for.

Firestar rose to his paws again and raised his tail for silence. The caterwauling gradually died away and the cats sat down again, directing angry glares at the RiverClan leader.

"I'm sure you have good reason for accusing us all like that," Firestar meowed when he could make himself heard. "Would you like to explain?"

ENTER THE WORLD OF WARRIORS

Warriors

Sinister perils threaten the four warrior Clans. Into the midst of this turmoil comes Rusty, an ordinary housecat, who may just be the bravest of them all.

Warriors: The New Prophecy

Follow the next generation of heroic cats as they set off on a quest to save the Clans from destruction.

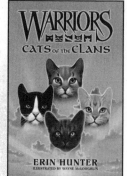

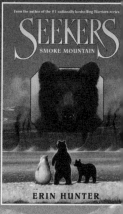